**What to Bee?**

**Written and Illustrated by Dee Smith**

**Copyright © 2016**

**Visit Deesignery.com**

You may not have wings to soar up high.

But here are some ways you can reach the sky.

Be creative.

Never give up on your dreams.

Your goals are closer than they may seem.

Be friendly and treat others with care.

Happiness is amazing to share.

Be polite wherever you go.

Your good manners are great to show.

Be yourself.

Love the special things about you.

There are so many things that you can do.

Most of all don't be afraid to try.

Face your fears and soar up high.

Being a bee,

It is a most lovely thing.

But to be amazing you don't need these wings.

Just be yourself in these special ways.

And just like me,

You'll enjoy wonderful days.

# Another adventure in Bee-ville to read next!

**A rhyming picture book about what to do if you feel bullied.**

## Thank You!

Thank you so much for reading this book.
It means the world to me!
If you liked the book I would much appreciate if you would write a Review on Amazon. I am so thankful for each and every person supporting my dream of being a writer for children. Because you have read this book, yes that means YOU too! Thanks Again!
Stay tuned for more titles on my website Deesignery.com

Regards,
Dee

## About the Author:

My name is Dee Smith. I am an Author and Illustrator. My hobbies include graphic design, puppetry, balloon twisting, drawing and of course writing. I am dedicated to my mission of keeping children entertained in fun and innovative ways.

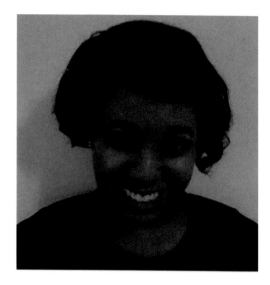

85911409R00015

Made in the USA
Middletown, DE
27 August 2018